P9-CKY-507

The Boxcar Children® Mysteries

The Pet Shop Mystery
The Mystery of the Secret Message
The Firehouse Mystery
The Mystery in San Francisco
The Niagara Falls Mystery
The Mystery at the Alamo
The Outer Space Mystery
The Soccer Mystery
The Mystery in the Old Attic
The Growling Bear Mystery
The Mystery of the Lake Monster
The Mystery at Peacock Hall
The Windy City Mystery
The Black Pearl Mystery
The Cereal Box Mystery
The Panther Mystery
The Mystery of the Queen's Jewels
The Mystery of the Stolen Sword
The Basketball Mystery
The Movie Star Mystery
The Mystery of the Black Raven
The Mystery of the Pirate's Map
The Mystery in the Mall
The Mystery in New York
The Gymnastics Mystery
The Poison Frog Mystery
The Great Bicycle Race Mystery
The Mystery of the Wild Ponies

THE MYSTERY OF THE WILD PONIES

created by
GERTRUDE CHANDLER WARNER

Illustrated by Hodges Soileau

ALBERT WHITMAN & Company
Morton Grove, Illinois

Library of Congress Cataloging-in-Publication Data
is available from the Library of Congress.

The Mystery of the Wild Ponies
created by Gertrude Chandler Warner;
illustrated by Hodges Soileau.

ISBN 0-8075-5465-0(hardcover)
ISBN 0-8075-5466-9(paperback)

Cover art by David Cunningham.

Contents

CHAPTER 1

A Vacation from Mysteries?

"Look at the water!" Benny Alden exclaimed happily as Grandfather drove the station wagon over the bridge. Below, blue-green water sparkled in the bright sunlight.

Ten-year-old Violet was excited, too. "Are we at the Outer Banks yet?"

"Not yet," said their grandfather, James Alden.

Fourteen-year-old Henry, who had been guiding Grandfather with a map, spoke to his little sister from the front seat. "Just over this long bridge, Violet, and we're there."

As they drove off the bridge and onto land again, Jessie Alden cheered, "Here we are!" Like the others in the family, she was looking forward to a vacation on an island off the coast of North Carolina.

At twelve, Jessie kept the Aldens organized on their many trips. Yesterday they left their home in Greenfield, Connecticut. They waved good-bye to their housekeeper, Mrs. McGregor, and to Watch, their dog, and began the long drive south.

Now they were on one of the islands that together are known as the Outer Banks. The two-lane road wound between thick bushes. Beyond the bushes the children caught glimpses of cozy houses.

Benny bounced in his seat. "I can't see the ocean, but I can smell it."

"I bet it's just over that long sandy hill," Violet said.

She breathed in the salty air. Benny was right. You could smell the ocean! Her brother was only six years old, but he was pretty smart.

Grandfather steered the station wagon into a crushed-oyster-shell parking lot and parked in front of a small building. OCEAN TIDES REALTY, read a bright sign above the door.

"Be back in a jiffy," he said. "I'm just getting the key to our cottage."

Benny leaned out the car window. Across the road was an ice-cream stand. "I wonder if they have fudge ripple," he said hopefully.

"Are you hungry already?" Jessie asked him. "We had a huge lunch in Elizabeth City."

"But that was *hours* ago," Benny said.

Just then Grandfather appeared with keys dangling from a wooden cut-out gull. He saw Benny staring at the ice-cream stand and everyone laughing.

"Let me guess, Benny," he said. "You're hungry!"

"Yes!" said Violet, Henry, and Jessie all at once.

James Alden shook his head. "Some things never change. Benny is always hungry. And you kids manage to solve a mystery on every trip we take."

"Mysteries just seem to find us," said Henry.

"We're on vacation for a week," said Grandfather. "Maybe we can take a vacation from mysteries, too."

Jessie glanced out the window: just sand and sky and pretty houses. This was the most unmysterious place she had ever seen. Grandfather would surely get his wish.

The station wagon turned into a driveway.

Henry looked at the weathered gray two-story house. Some cottage! The house was big, with lots of windows, and upper and lower wraparound decks. And it was built on wooden pilings, which looked like stilts.

Grandfather pulled the car into a space under the house. "Welcome to Gullwing Cottage," he said.

Benny hopped out of the car. "Cool!" he

exclaimed. "It's like a tree house, but without the tree!"

"Well, we lived in a boxcar once," said Henry, "so this isn't so strange."

The Alden children never forgot the time they lived in an abandoned railway car. Their parents had died and they had no place to go until Grandfather found them and took them to his big house in Greenfield. He even had the boxcar towed to their backyard so they could play in it.

"The houses here are built on pilings because of hurricanes and big storms," explained Grandfather. "Basements would flood. The houses are built up so high water flows underneath."

"I hope we don't have a hurricane this week," Jessie said, hauling luggage from the trunk.

"The weather report says we should have clear skies," said Violet. She picked up the backpack that contained her art supplies. She loved to draw and paint, and she hoped to make lots of pictures while she was here.

Jessie and Violet decided to share a large room with an ocean view. Henry and Benny claimed the room next door because it had two sets of bunk beds. They could each sleep in the top bunk. Grandfather chose a sunny room with a view of the Sound.

"Thank goodness we have a kitchen," Benny said, eagerly opening the refrigerator. His face fell when he saw it was empty.

Jessie laughed. "We have to go to the grocery store, Benny. We'll buy lots of things you like to eat!"

But before they got in the car again, Grandfather suggested everyone relax a few moments.

The children went out on the upper deck, where they could see all the way to the bright blue ocean.

"There's the dune." Henry pointed to a steep hill of sand that sloped on its far side down to the Atlantic. On the beach, a boy flew a blue-and-yellow kite. Two surfers braved the tumbling waves.

"That looks like fun," said Henry. He

hoped to try surfing while he was here.

Gullwing Cottage was flanked by other houses. Bright beach towels were draped over the deck rail of the three-story house on one side. A narrow boardwalk, like a sidewalk, connected the houses.

A sandy-haired boy stepped outside of the brown-shingled house on the other side. When he saw the Aldens, he waved. Even from a distance the Aldens could tell he was a lot older than Henry.

"C'mon over!" he called.

"Let's go meet him!" said Benny.

They went back inside and told Grandfather they would be next door meeting their neighbor.

The older boy was waiting for them on the boardwalk between the two houses. The boardwalk also crossed over the dune.

"Hey," he said in a friendly voice. "I'm Jeremy Ross."

"Pleased to meet you," said Henry. He introduced his brother and sisters. "Are you here with your family?"

Jeremy shook his head. "My roommates and I are students at the University of North Carolina."

Violet thought Jeremy was cute, with his blue eyes and deep dimples. Shyly, she asked, "What are you studying?"

"You mean what is my major?" Jeremy's eyes danced. "According to my roommates, Paul and Drew, I'm majoring in practical jokes!"

Benny was delighted. "You can take that in school?"

Jeremy playfully rumpled Benny's hair. "Not officially. But I've pulled some good stunts. This morning I woke up Drew with a large bucket of water!"

Jessie didn't think that was so funny, but she couldn't help liking Jeremy. She loved his southern accent.

Jeremy noticed that Benny was dreamily watching the blue-and-yellow kite bob overhead. "Do you like to fly kites?" he asked Benny.

"I sure do!" said Benny.

"I'm a kite flier from way back," Jeremy

replied. "Maybe we'll fly some kites to-gether."

"Thanks, but we've got to go," Jessie told Jeremy. "We just arrived and we need to get some stuff at the store."

As they left, they saw a dark-haired woman standing on the deck of the three-story house. She squinted at them from beneath the brim of a straw hat.

"That's our other neighbor," said Benny. "Let's go meet her, too!"

Before anyone could stop him, Benny scampered across the sandy yard to the top of the flight of steps leading up to the woman's deck.

An easel was set up by the sliding glass door. The woman was carrying a canvas under one arm. She struggled to pick up a large tackle box with the other hand.

Benny bounded up the steps to her. "Can I help?" he asked.

"Who are you?" demanded the woman. Under the hat brim, her dark eyes glinted with suspicion.

"I'm Benny Alden," he answered. "We

live next door. Are you an artist, too? My sister is an artist."

"I don't have time to chat, little boy. I'm losing my best light," said the woman.

Henry was right behind Benny.

"Is this your brother?" the woman asked him, clearly annoyed.

"I'm sorry," Henry apologized. "Benny's only six years old and I guess being at the beach has him all excited."

Jessie and Violet joined Henry. When Violet saw the art supplies, her heart skipped a beat. A real artist was staying right next door!

After Henry introduced them, the woman reluctantly told them her name was Winifred Gorman.

"Do you paint with oils or watercolors?" asked Violet with interest.

"Both. When I still have proper light. If you kids don't mind, I really must go," Winifred said.

"We'll help carry your things down to the beach, if that's where you're going," Benny offered.

"I'm just going up on the dune. I can handle it myself," Winifred said brusquely. "I always have."

As the Aldens turned to leave, she leaned over the rail.

"When did you get here?" she asked sharply.

Jessie turned back to reply. "A little while ago. Why?"

"Somebody stole one of my beach towels last night." Winifred frowned at them. "I guess it couldn't have been any of you."

When they were inside Gullwing Cottage again, Jessie said, "I can't believe it! She practically accused us of stealing!"

"She wasn't very nice," Violet agreed, disappointed. She hoped to make friends with the artist next door. But Winifred Gorman didn't seem the friendly type.

"I wonder who stole Ms. Gorman's beach towel?" Benny wondered.

Jessie put her hands on her hips. "It probably blew away in the wind. We're not looking for any mysteries, remember?"

"I don't know where we'd find one,"

Henry said, gazing out the window. "This seems like the quietest place we've ever been."

"Good," said James Alden, coming into the room. "I hope it stays that way!"

"Are we going to the grocery store now?" Violet wanted to know.

"I did some checking," said Grandfather. "The closest grocery store is in Corolla, several miles up the road. But there's a small market close by. I'll drive over now and get a few things there for breakfast. You children can stay and settle in. Tomorrow we'll all do our main shopping."

"What about supper?" Benny asked, hungry as always.

"We'll eat out tonight," Grandfather said.

"Sounds good," said Jessie.

But Benny was too hungry to wait for dinner. As soon as Grandfather came back with the groceries, he fixed his favorite sandwich — peanut butter, banana, and mayonnaise on white bread. He carried the snack outside on the lower deck, then realized he'd forgotten his drink.

When Benny returned with a can of soda, his sandwich was gone!

"Hey!" he exclaimed.

The other children came running.

"What happened?" Henry asked.

Benny pointed to the railing where he had left the paper plate. "I set my sandwich right there and went inside to get a drink. When I came back, it was gone!"

Jessie walked down the ramp. "Here's the plate," she reported.

"Where's my sandwich?" Benny asked.

Henry had been scanning the blue sky. "You know what I think?" he said. "I think those gulls took your sandwich, Benny."

Benny was amazed. "Birds flew off with a whole sandwich?"

"Seagulls are scavengers," Henry added. "They eat garbage, fish — just about anything. Your sandwich was probably a real treat."

"I sure hope they enjoyed it," Benny said.

The others went back inside. Benny started to follow, but then he thought of something. He walked down the ramp and checked where the paper plate had fallen. There were wide, deep marks in the sand. If seagulls took his sandwich, they wouldn't have left tracks like those!

Something a lot bigger than a bird had stolen his sandwich, Benny was sure.

CHAPTER 2

The Ghost Horse

"We're going someplace special for dinner," Grandfather announced.

Eagerly the children climbed into the car. The long trip and the salty air had made them all hungry. As Grandfather swung the station wagon onto the road, Jessie noticed a sign she hadn't seen before.

It showed a silhouette of a horse and read, SLOW! HORSE CROSSING. She couldn't recall seeing any stables nearby, only houses.

Moments later, Grandfather turned in to

a wide driveway. Low, gray-shingled buildings with balconies faced the ocean. A sleek seagull was carved into the double doors of the main entrance. Violet noticed that the seagull had been carved using only one line. After dinner when they were back at the cottage, she would try copying that single-line bird, she told herself.

"Where are we?" she asked.

Grandfather drove past tennis courts and a glittering pool to an older building. "This is the Seagull Resort," he replied. "It's the only resort in the Outer Banks."

Henry watched a couple in crisp tennis outfits walk off the courts. "This place is too fancy. I like our house better."

"I prefer peace and quiet at the beach, but some people like a lot of organized activity," said Grandfather. "The resort has a restaurant, though."

"Just as long as they have food," said Benny.

As they went inside, his eyes lit up. "Oh, boy!" he exclaimed.

"It's like the inside of a boat," Jessie remarked, staring at the thick ropes and huge old-fashioned pulleys in a glass case.

"It used to be a lifesaving station," Grandfather replied. "There are several of these stations up and down the Outer Banks. This is the only one restored as a restaurant."

The headwaiter led them to a table by one of the large windows.

Henry began reading a brief history of the lifesaving stations printed on the back of his menu. "It says here the Outer Banks used to be dangerous to ships."

The waiter, who was filling their water glasses, nodded. "This area was once called the 'Graveyard of the Atlantic.' During storms, ships were driven into the shallow waters and often wrecked."

"How awful!" Violet commented.

"Yes, it was," said the waiter. "Many men lost their lives. So in 1874 the U.S. Lifesaving Service was started. The government built seven stations. This is number five, built in 1899."

"So exactly what did the rescuers do?" asked Jessie.

"A lot," said the waiter. "The men worked all winter in icy waters, standing watch on the shore. When the rescuers spotted a grounded ship, they hauled their equipment down to the beach in carts pulled by the island's wild ponies, some of which were caught and tamed for this job," the waiter added. "Then they'd row out to the ship and bring the stranded crew to shore. It was hard, dangerous work."

Benny was fascinated. "I want to be a rescuer, too!"

Their waiter smiled. "You can, when you grow up. The Lifesaving Service is now the U.S. Coast Guard." He poised his pencil over his pad. "I've been talking too much. Do you know what you'd like?"

Grandfather ordered swordfish steak, while Jessie and Henry asked for the Carolina barbecue. Violet and Benny chose cheeseburgers with the works.

As they waited for their food, they wandered around the restaurant, which was decorated with old photographs and lifesaving gear. Jessie lingered by a picture of a crew of surfmen posed by their carts and boats. The rescuers all wore handlebar mustaches and serious expressions. One man held the bridle of a shaggy pony. Didn't the waiter mention something about wild ponies?

Crash!

The sound of shattered dishes came from the kitchen. Voices raised in argument were heard all the way in the dining room.

Jessie recognized their waiter's voice as she and the others returned to their table. Their waiter was obviously angry. The other voice sounded apologetic.

The waiter appeared just then, carrying a tray with the iced teas Grandfather had ordered.

"I'm very sorry," he said to the Aldens. "A young man wanted to apply for a job as a busboy. I told him he was too inexperienced, but he insisted on lifting a heavy tray. You heard the result." He smiled and left again.

The incident was forgotten when their food arrived. After a dessert of apple cobbler with ice cream, they drove back to Gullwing Cottage.

"It's still early," Benny said. "Can we take a walk?"

"Good idea," said Grandfather, though he decided to stay behind to read. "Why don't you go see the landward part of the island," he suggested.

"The landward part?" asked Benny. "What is that?"

Grandfather smiled. "This island is long and narrow. Our cottage is on the seaward side, which faces the open ocean, where the waves are big. The landward side of the island faces the Carolina coast. The bridge we drove over earlier today connects North Carolina to the landward side. The water is much calmer on that side and there are docks full of fishing boats."

"Docks? Boats?" said Benny. "Let's go!"

The main road was busy, but the children crossed safely. They found a wooden walk that led to the docks.

Violet caught her breath when she saw

the orange sun resting on the horizon. What a great spot to paint!

"Look!" Benny cried. He pointed to a large brown bird perched on one of the pilings near an older man.

The man sat on an upturned bait bucket at the end of the dock. He was untangling fishing line. The Aldens walked out to him.

"Excuse me," said Jessie. "Is that your pelican?"

The older man laughed. "He thinks he's mine. Out here every day, rain or shine, hopin' to grab my catch."

"Are you a fisherman?" asked Violet. With his gray hair, bright blue eyes, and fisherman's cap, the man looked as at home on the pier as the pelican.

"I do a little fishin'. I catch a few crabs." The crinkles around his eyes deepened. "You young folks on vacation?"

"Yes, sir." Henry introduced the others and explained that they were staying a week at Gullwing Cottage. "You're from here, aren't you?" he guessed.

"Born and raised here. Name's Shad Toler."

"Shad?" asked Benny. "Is that a name?"

Jessie nudged her brother. "Benny!"

"It's a nickname," said Shad. "Shad is a kind of fish. My real name is Rupert. I was never fond of it, though. Shad suits me just fine."

"Have you always lived on the island?" asked Violet.

Shad nodded. "Yes. I never saw a reason to leave. Got a piece of land here. People been after me for years to sell. I could make a lot of money if I sold it. But I won't sell. I don't need a lot of money. Long as I can fish a little, I'm happy."

Henry looked along the shoreline. There were lots of houses on this side of the island.

"I bet this place has changed since you were a boy," he observed.

"Yeah. Can't stand in the way of progress," said Shad. "I remember when we didn't have telephones here. I still don't have one hooked up. And I went to school in a one-room schoolhouse."

"Everybody in just one room?" Benny asked. It sounded very crowded.

Shad grinned. "At recess, we'd all run up on the dune. It was bigger then. We'd play catch or five-oh. I think you call it hide-and-seek."

Jessie imagined growing up on an island. It must have been so much fun!

"But best of all," Shad said, "were the wild horses."

"Wild horses!" Benny exclaimed. "Are there wild horses here?"

Shad laughed at Benny's expression. "Haven't you seen them? Guess not. The herd pretty much stays north of here, in that new pony pen." He shook his head. "A shame. Wild animals ought to be free, not locked up."

"Why are they in a pen?" Jessie asked, shocked.

Shad shrugged. "Safer, so they say. The horses like to roam. But they cross that road. In the last few years, some have been hit by cars."

"How sad!" said Violet. She hated the idea of any animal being hurt.

"They built this pen to keep the horses from runnin' around. I don't like the idea myself, but it's supposed to be best for the horses," said Shad.

"Can we go see the horses?" Benny wanted to know.

"You can drive up there," Shad replied. "Sometimes you get lucky and see them, sometimes not." Then he lowered his voice and peered at them from under his bushy brows. "But if you're real lucky, you might see a particular horse."

Jessie leaned forward. "Which one?"

"Name's Magic. Used to be the leader of the herd."

"Used to be?" asked Henry. "What happened?"

The wind had picked up. Shad gazed out at the choppy waters. Whitecaps danced on the waves.

"Magic was hit by a car one foggy night,"

he said. "Poor animal was killed instantly."

Violet felt a shiver trickle down her spine. "But people can still see him?"

"Yes," said Shad. "On certain moonlit nights, if you're real lucky, you might see the ghost of Magic, runnin' along the beach. He's come back to take over his herd."

CHAPTER 3

What Benny Saw

"A ghost horse!" Benny said excitedly as they walked back to Gullwing Cottage. "Neat!"

"Now, Benny," Jessie said gently. "It's just a story. I bet Mr. Toler likes to tell stories."

"But it could be true," Benny insisted.

Violet silently agreed with her little brother, even though she knew ghosts didn't exist. She could imagine the shimmery horse prancing in the moonlight.

Home again, the children realized they

were tired after the long day. Everyone went to bed early.

In the room he shared with Henry, Benny lay in the top bunk across from his brother and listened to the surf outside. Henry was already asleep.

Benny thought about climbing down the bunk bed ladder to look out the window. Maybe he'd see Magic, the ghost horse. He'd get down right now, but first he'd just close his eyes for a moment. . . .

Instead of moonlight, Benny woke to bright sunshine beaming in his face and the delicious aroma of frying bacon.

"Hey, sleepyhead," Henry greeted his little brother. He was wearing shorts and a T-shirt. "Jessie says breakfast is almost ready."

Benny didn't need to be told twice. He was dressed and sitting at the round oak table in a flash.

Jessie and Grandfather served toasted English muffins, scrambled eggs, bacon, and orange juice.

"After we've cleaned up," said Grandfather, "we'll drive to that grocery store in Corolla and buy food for the week."

Henry took the big cooler out to the car, for milk and meat that might spoil. When the dishes were done, they all got into the station wagon.

The road twisted north for several miles. Then Benny spotted a redbrick lighthouse towering over the trees.

"Look!" he cried.

"That's the Currituck Beach Lighthouse," Grandfather said. "It's the only lighthouse this far north on the Outer Banks. Because this strip of land is so narrow, storms and hurricanes often do lots of damage."

"What about all these houses?" Violet noticed huge houses on either side of the road.

"Good question," said Grandfather. "If they are built too close to the ocean, they could be swept out to sea in a really powerful storm."

They drove to a shopping center with a large grocery store and, with everyone helping, they got everything they needed in a few minutes.

At the checkout counter, Grandfather added a copy of the local newspaper. Henry loaded the heavy bags into the back of the car. As they were pulling out, he saw a sign.

" 'The Corolla Wild Horse Sanctuary,' " Henry exclaimed. "That must be where the wild horses are kept."

"Can we go see them, Grandfather?" Benny asked.

"Of course. I've heard about these horses but have never seen them."

The road went from pavement to gravel and then they arrived at a gate that barred the way.

Violet was disappointed. "I guess we can't go in after all."

A uniformed young man with freckles and red hair was locking the gate. When he heard their car, he turned and smiled.

"Hello," he said in a friendly way. "You can get out of the car and watch from the gate if you like."

"We were hoping to see the wild horses," Grandfather said.

The officer glanced back toward the high dune topped with sea grass. "I only saw a few of them myself this morning. The rest must be on the far side of the sanctuary." He put out a hand. "I'm Officer Thomas Hyde."

"Are you a policeman?" Benny asked in awe, shaking the man's hand.

Officer Hyde grinned. "Sanctuary officer. My job is to take care of the horses. I stop traffic if the herd crosses the road, and prevent people from feeding or trying to pet or ride the horses."

"I thought the horses were penned in," Henry said. "How can they cross the road?"

Officer Hyde pointed to the fence on either side of the gate. "Horses naturally want to roam to new grazing areas. They swim around the fence on the ocean side. We can't fence in the ocean."

"What happens if the horses get out?" Jessie wanted to know.

"I find them," said Officer Hyde. "I'm in radio contact with the sheriff's office and an on-call vet. Mainly I protect the herd from tourists. It's against the law to bother these animals, you know."

Benny was hanging on the gate. "I see them!" he cried. "Here they come!"

Officer Hyde shaded his eyes from the glare of the sun. "This is your lucky day. Once in a while the horses follow me to the gate."

Violet held her breath as she waited for the herd to come into view.

At last several horses ambled over the dune. They were small, with shaggy manes and tails. Most were a reddish-brown color, though some were spotted with white. A couple were coal-black.

"How cute!" Jessie exclaimed. "They look like ponies!"

"Many people call them ponies," said Officer Hyde. "But they are true descendants of Spanish mustangs. They aren't that small, really. Most are thirteen to fourteen hands high."

Benny frowned, holding out his palms. "Hands?"

Officer Hyde laughed. "It's an old, easy way to measure things. A hand equals four inches. Horses are generally eighteen hands high."

"Here, sweetie." Violet tried to coax over a chestnut-brown horse with a white face. The horse had big brown eyes fringed with long lashes.

"Please remember these are not friendly animals," Officer Hyde warned her. "They look cute, but they may bite and kick."

They watched the horses nibble on grass. Officer Hyde told them there were actually two pony herds on the Outer Banks. The other herd was penned on Okracoke Island. When more people started coming to the Banks, the herd split and migrated to the northern and southern ends, he explained as he glanced at his watch.

Grandfather smiled. "You must have other duties. Thanks for talking to us."

"Anytime," said Officer Hyde, walking over to his Jeep. "Here's a brochure about the sanctuary. You can reach me at the lighthouse if you have any more questions."

The kids waved good-bye.

"He's nice," said Violet.

Benny agreed. "I want to be a pony policeman."

"What about the Coast Guard?" Henry teased.

"That, too." Benny planned to have lots of jobs when he grew up.

At the cottage, they unpacked the groceries. Henry picked up the newspaper.

"Here's a story about the ponies," he said.

The others gathered around the table. Henry held up the newspaper and read the story aloud. They learned that the horses were brought to the island in 1523 by Spanish explorers and that there were only nineteen horses in the Corolla herd.

"No wonder they are special," Violet commented. "But it's sad so many have been hit by cars."

"That's why the sanctuary was started," said Jessie. "It seems mean to pen them up, but at least they're safer."

Benny was looking at the pictures in the newspaper as the others talked about wild ponies. *Wow,* he thought, *what is that?* It was a picture of some kids at summer camp, but one of the boys wore a necklace with one large, sharp, triangle-shaped tooth hanging from it. Benny wondered what kind of tooth it was and where he might find one, until his stomach started grumbling and his thoughts turned to food.

The kids fixed a quick lunch of turkey sandwiches, apple juice, and cookies. Then they changed into bathing suits and walked over the dune to the beach.

First they splashed in the waves. Then they wet some sand above the high-tide line and built a huge castle. Next they hunted for shells.

Jessie spied a familiar figure on the dune behind them. "There's Winifred Gorman. She's painting."

"Oh, let's go see!" said Benny.

He ran off before Jessie could stop him. Jessie knew some artists didn't like other people peering at their work. Winifred

Gorman did not seem happy to see the Aldens.

"I'm not on public display," she said grumpily. "I'm working." She tossed her brush down with a sigh.

Violet studied the seascape. "It's very nice, only — "

"Only what?" Winifred said sharply.

"It's just waves and beach," Violet said nervously. "Maybe you could put in some people or animals. Like the wild horses."

Winifred considered her suggestion. "Hmmm. I forgot about those wild ponies. My real estate agent mentioned them when I bought this house."

"You live here?" Benny wanted to know.

"No, not year-round. I live in New York City. This is my first summer here." She became impatient again. "Where are those ponies you mentioned? I must paint them while the light is good."

Henry pointed north. "The sanctuary is that way. You can't miss it."

The artist snatched her canvas off the

easel, grabbed her tackle box of paints and brushes, and hurried off.

The children were stretched out on their deck when they heard Winifred Gorman's car pull into the driveway next door.

Benny ran to the railing. "Did you see the ponies?" he called.

Her car door slammed angrily. "No, I did not," she said stiffly. "I drove all the way up there and stood outside that stupid gate for ages. But did any of them show up? No!"

"We saw them this morning," said Violet. "They're really cute."

"Well, that makes me feel better," Winifred said sharply. "How am I going to paint a horse I can't see?" The artist stomped up the steps into her house.

"Boy, is she grouchy," Benny commented.

"She just wants to paint a good picture," Violet said. "Mmm! What's that smell?"

Benny knew that smell. "Hamburgers!"

Grandfather was grilling hamburgers on the deck. Jessie added potato salad, applesauce, and a coconut cake from the store bakery.

Full and pleasantly tired from their day in the sun, the Aldens once again went to bed early.

Benny and Henry chatted awhile.

"What will happen to my sand castle?" Benny asked.

"The tide might wash it away," Henry replied, yawning. "But we can build another one tomorrow." Then he fell asleep.

Benny lay awake, thinking about his sand castle. He wondered if he could see it from the window. Was the moat filled with water?

Climbing down the ladder, he dropped softly to the floor. He didn't want to wake Henry.

The window was open, letting in the sound of the surf. Benny leaned on the sill, straining to see in the darkness.

A silver-dollar moon had risen above the ocean, shining on the beach. Benny noticed a light still on in Winifred Gorman's house.

Was she looking at the moon, too? he wondered.

Suddenly Benny heard a strange cry. It sounded like it came from the dune! As he turned his head, he caught a glimpse of something on the beach.

It was a horse, its shiny coat gleaming in the pale moonlight. The animal pawed the sand, nodding its proud head. Then it cantered out of sight down the beach.

Benny swallowed. "Magic," he whispered. "The famous ghost horse."

CHAPTER 4

"Don't Tell Grandfather!"

"I saw Magic," Benny declared the next morning.

The other children stopped fixing breakfast and stared at him. Grandfather had left for an early-morning exercise class at the Seagull Resort.

"You saw what?" asked Henry.

"Magic, the ghost horse. He was on the beach. And I heard a cry."

"The horse cried?" Violet set bowls of granola and sliced peaches on the table.

"No," said Benny. "It sounded like a person. But I didn't see anybody. Only the horse."

Jessie frowned as she brought over a pitcher of cold milk. "Benny, are you sure you weren't dreaming?"

"I got up to look at my sand castle. I saw a horse. It has to be the ghost horse Shad told us about," he insisted.

"There's one way to solve this," said Henry. "After breakfast, we'll go down to the beach and check for prints in the sand. If the tide's right, they won't have been washed away."

Benny had never eaten so fast. He wanted to prove he had really seen the ghost horse.

When the bowls and glasses were rinsed, the kids headed outside.

It was a great morning. The sun was shining brightly over the slate-blue ocean. A man with a metal detector swept the beach, looking for coins and jewelry. Benny's sand castle was still there, untouched.

Nearby, where Benny had wet the sand to build his castle, the kids saw the fresh shoe prints of a jogger.

Benny's heart dropped. Suppose the jogger messed up the horse's prints.

Then Violet exclaimed, "Look!" She pointed to a small, scooped impression in the sand.

Henry let out a low whistle. "Here's another one. Benny was right. A horse was definitely on our beach."

"I think we should call Officer Hyde," said Jessie. "He'll know for certain."

They ran back to the cottage and phoned the lighthouse. Officer Hyde answered and said he would be there shortly.

Violet remembered Grandfather would be having a late breakfast at the Seagull Resort with the rest of his class.

"Let's not mention it to Grandfather," she said. "He said he wanted a vacation from mysteries anyway."

"We didn't go looking for this mystery," Henry put in. "It found us!"

When Thomas Hyde arrived, he was eager to see the hoofprints. The children led him to the beach and the trail of prints.

The sanctuary officer knelt down to study

the impressions. "These are definitely the tracks of a horse, maybe even a stallion," he said. "And you said you saw the horse?"

"Last night," Benny replied. "Maybe it was the ghost of that horse that was killed."

Thomas straightened up with a sigh and a smile. "So you've heard the legend of Magic. Benny, I believe you saw a horse. But ghost horses wouldn't leave tracks."

"Benny heard someone cry, too," added Violet. "But he didn't see anyone."

"Horses don't cry," said Officer Hyde. "I think one of the horses got out of the pen and came down here. He's probably back in the herd."

When Officer Hyde left, the children discussed what they had learned.

"Our vacation won't be mystery-free," said Violet.

Benny squinted in the sun. He saw a man with a fishing pole standing knee-deep in water farther down the beach. "Isn't that Shad?"

"Just the person we want to see," said

Henry. "Maybe he'll tell us more about this ghost horse."

They walked down the beach to meet Shad.

"Hey," he said, giving the traditional island greeting. "How are y'all this mornin'?"

"Fine," answered Jessie. "Catch anything yet?"

"Naw. Blues are runnin', but they don't like me today!" He gave his gruff laugh.

"Guess what," said Benny. "I saw a horse last night."

Shad's eyes widened. "You don't say. On the beach? It must have been Magic."

"We found hoofprints in the sand," added Henry. "The sanctuary officer saw them, too."

"That young horse fella?" Shad frowned. "He's okay. But I wish they'd forget about that fence nonsense and let the horses roam free like they used to."

"But they get hit by cars," said Violet. "That's what happened to Magic."

"Get rid of the cars," Shad said simply.

"Make people take a ferry here and walk or ride a bicycle anyplace they want to go."

"Benny also heard a cry, like a person," Henry said.

"That bridge connecting us to the mainland has ruined this island," Shad said. He shook his head. "It brings in too many people, too many cars."

Henry realized they weren't going to find out more from the fisherman. Shad was only interested in talking about the island. "We've got to go," he said.

"See you around," Shad said with a wave. "Come visit me on the dock anytime. If I'm not there, I'll be on the beach."

As the Aldens crossed over the dune, Jessie made a suggestion.

"Let's talk to our neighbors. Maybe Winifred Gorman or the college boys saw Benny's horse," she said.

"Ms. Gorman's light was on last night!" said Benny, remembering.

Winifred Gorman was sitting on her deck, having a cup of tea. She didn't seem pleased to see them.

"May we come up?" Henry asked.

"Might as well," the artist replied.

The children climbed the deck steps. Winifred didn't offer them a seat at her umbrella table, so they stood by the rail.

"We wanted to ask you a question," said Jessie.

"Ask away." The woman seemed irritated.

"Did you see a horse last night?" said Benny. "On the beach?"

Winifred stared at him from under her hat brim. "A horse on the beach? How could I see that? I was in bed."

"I saw your light on," Benny said.

"So? Lots of people leave lights on. That doesn't mean I was up looking at horses or whatever."

From where she was standing, Violet was able to see in the wide sliding glass doors. A painting rested on an easel in Winifred's airy living room.

The painting showed a black stallion on a dune.

"Is that all?" Winifred was saying. "If you don't mind, I have work to do."

"Thanks," Henry said, leading them off the deck. "We won't bother you anymore."

On the way to the college boys' house, Violet told the others what she had seen.

"Where did that painting come from?" Jessie wanted to know. "Yesterday she was mad because none of the horses showed up to model for her. Could she have seen what Benny saw?"

"Maybe she copied the horse from a picture," Violet said. "Artists do that sometimes. But how did she paint it so fast?"

Those were questions the children couldn't answer. Maybe the boys next door would have more information.

Jeremy Ross was rinsing sand off his bodysurfing board. He turned the hose off when he saw the Aldens.

"Hey there," he said, glad to see them. "I was just going in for a snack. Want to join me?"

The kids followed him into the kitchen. Jessie muffled a giggle when she saw the mess. Empty pizza boxes, soda cans, and chips bags littered the counter. It didn't take a detective to see three messy college kids lived here!

"Where are Drew and Paul?" asked Henry.

"Still surfing. I'm afraid they're going to get waterlogged," said Jeremy. He pulled a loaf of bread and a jar of mayonnaise from the refrigerator. A bowl of bananas sat on the counter. The Aldens watched Jeremy make peanut butter, mayonnaise, and banana sandwiches.

"Hey! That's my favorite!" Benny exclaimed. And, he thought, that was the same sandwich that disappeared from their deck.

"Mine, too," said Jeremy. "Guys come into my dorm room all the time for a Ross Special. That's what they call it."

He asked if they were hungry and quickly slapped together five gooey sandwiches. Benny bit into his with delight.

"By the way," Jessie began, "did you happen to see a horse last night?"

Jeremy poured them all glasses of milk. "A horse? The only thing I saw was the inside of my eyelids," he joked. "I was asleep."

"We were just wondering." Henry finished his sandwich.

Jeremy didn't seem interested. "Did I ever tell you guys about the big stunt I pulled last semester?"

Benny shook his head. "What was it?"

"I'm surprised you didn't read about it in the papers," the older boy crowed. "It was that great."

"What did you do?" asked Violet, curious.

Jeremy grinned teasingly. "Tell you someday."

Jessie picked up their plates and glasses. Jeremy obviously liked to tease. "We should go," she told him. "Our grandfather will be home soon."

"Come back anytime," Jeremy said, opening the door. "Maybe I'll tell you about the Greatest Stunt in the World."

"He's fun," said Violet as they crossed the wooden walkway. "I wonder what he did."

"I bet Jeremy is still pulling stunts," observed Henry. "He could have taken Ms. Gorman's towel."

"And my sandwich," Benny added. "We both like the same kind."

Jessie wasn't listening. She was watching a boy with hair so blond it was nearly white. The boy carried a beach chair down the road. Stenciled on the blue canvas back was a bird. She'd seen that bird somewhere.

"Look at that boy," she said to the others. "Where could he be going with a chair?"

Henry shaded his eyes. "That bird design looks familiar."

"It's just like the sign at the Seagull Resort," Violet said. Last night she'd practiced drawing a bird with one line.

"Violet's right!" said Jessie. "But where is he going? The resort is down the road. Why would he carry a chair all the way up here?"

"Maybe it got washed up on the beach," Benny offered.

Henry shook his head. "The current brings things south, not north. The chair would have been found south of here and he's walking from the north. Whoever he is, he didn't find that chair around here."

CHAPTER 5

The Horsenapper

"I'll pick you up in about twenty minutes," said Grandfather.

The children scrambled out of the station wagon. When Grandfather said at breakfast that he needed to pick up some items he'd forgotten at the grocery store, the children leaped at the chance to visit the wild horse sanctuary again.

"We'll be right here," Henry said to Grandfather. He noticed Thomas Hyde's Jeep parked outside the gate.

When Grandfather drove off, the Aldens walked up the sandy road.

Benny climbed on the gate. "No horses," he said, disappointed.

"Maybe they'll follow Officer Hyde back here like they did the other day," said Jessie.

They didn't have to wait long to see the sanctuary officer. He came down the path and opened the gate, then closed it behind him.

"You guys are up early," he said.

"We came to visit the horses while our grandfather is at the store," said Henry. Then he remembered a question he wanted to ask. "Did you see a lady here the other day? An artist? She always wears a big straw hat."

Officer Hyde shook his head. "I didn't see her. Did she want to see me?"

"She's our neighbor," Jessie replied. "She was trying to paint the horses. She was mad when they didn't show up."

Officer Hyde fumbled with the padlock, clearly upset. "They're wild animals. They don't care about human schedules."

Violet sensed something was wrong. "Is everything okay?" she asked, concerned.

"One of the horses is missing," Officer Hyde said.

"Missing!" Benny gasped.

Officer Hyde nodded. "Yes. At first I thought Midnight had simply wandered away from the herd. But I searched the sanctuary yesterday and this morning. I can't find him."

"Maybe he got out," said Jessie. "You said they do that sometimes."

"They do, but not for very long. You see, Midnight is the leader of the herd. Last week I noticed another stallion acting aggressive."

Benny frowned. "What do you mean?"

"There can only be one leader of a herd," Officer Hyde explained. "If another stallion wants to take over, he'll fight the leader. I think that's what happened. Midnight got in a fight and lost. He was driven away from the herd."

"Does that mean Midnight can't come back?" Henry asked.

"No. Midnight could take over again. But he can't be gone too long or the herd will accept the new leader instead." Officer Hyde gazed over the dune. "In any case, I need to find him. He may be injured."

"I guess Midnight is black," said Benny. He thought of the horse he'd seen pawing the beach the other night.

"Like midnight," Officer Hyde said, smiling. "Listen, if you kids see or hear anything, please let me know immediately. The sooner we find him, the better chance he has of regaining his place in the herd."

"What happens if he doesn't?" Violet asked, feeling sorry for the lost horse.

"It means he'd have to find a new herd," said Officer Hyde, opening the door to his Jeep. "That would be hard since the herd is so small. There are only a few new colts born every year."

"We'll be on the lookout," Henry promised.

Officer Hyde climbed in and drove off.

"I wonder where Midnight could be,"

Violet said. "We know it can't be the horse Benny saw on the beach that night."

"Mine was a ghost," Benny insisted. Then he had a thought. "What if Magic the ghost horse is the horse that had a fight with Midnight?"

"How could that be?" asked Henry gently. "Officer Hyde said he knew the other stallion that was trying to take over."

Benny wasn't about to let go of his idea. "But Shad told us Magic appeared when he wanted to go back to his herd."

Violet nodded. "That's right. Shad said when we see Magic, he'll be coming back to reclaim his rightful place in the herd." She quickly added, "But it's just a story, Benny."

"There are no ghosts," said Henry firmly. "Not even ghost horses."

At that moment, something whinnied behind him. Startled, the kids spun around.

"Oh, look!" Violet said softly.

Three horses stood at the gate, shaking their shaggy heads. Two of the ponies bent

to crop the grass growing at the base of the
gate. The third horse gazed at the kids.

"Such big brown eyes," said Jessie, fascinated. "It's like she's telling us something."

"I know what she's saying," Benny said.
"She wants Midnight back." Then he spoke
louder, so the horses could hear. "We'll find
him. We promise."

Henry smiled at his little brother's en-
thusiasm. He realized how important it was
to find the missing stallion. The Outer
Banks might look small on the map, but the
island they were on was actually fairly big.
Midnight could be anywhere.

When they got back to the cottage, the
kids changed into their suits and went down
to the beach. Henry carried a cooler of
drinks and snacks. Jessie brought a blue-
and-white-striped umbrella. Violet brought
her art things, the towels, and a sack of toys
for Benny.

They found a nice spot between the dune
and the ocean. Violet laid out the towels.

Henry stabbed the umbrella into the sand and opened it. Then he yelled, "Last one in the water is a rotten egg!"

With screams of laughter, the Aldens plunged into the waves. Jessie and Henry took Benny's hands and led him past the breakers. He squealed with delight as they played in the gently swelling waves.

Farther out, they saw Jeremy and his roommates bodysurfing, and Benny waved and shouted hello.

Jeremy yelled hello back to them and caught the next wave in. He landed at the foamy water's edge next to Benny.

"Hey," he greeted them, "do you want me to show you how to catch waves?"

"Yes!" they all cheered at once.

Jeremy coached Benny in the water close to the shore and gave Violet, Jessie, and Henry tips on catching the swells a little farther out.

While stopping together to catch their breath, Benny remembered something he'd wanted to ask their friendly college neighbor.

"Jeremy, you never told us about your big stunt," Benny said. "What was it?"

Jeremy grinned at the memory of his last big practical joke. "I 'borrowed' a goat from the veterinary department and dressed him up in my English professor's hat and scarf."

Benny laughed and Henry, Jessie, and Violet couldn't help smiling, even though they didn't approve of the prank.

When the kids grew tired of riding the waves, they thanked Jeremy and walked back up the beach. They wrapped themselves in thick, fluffy towels and sat in the sun to dry.

Suddenly Henry gave a cry. "Look! Dolphins!"

"Where?" Benny demanded. Then he saw their dark gray glistening bodies arch out of the water.

The Aldens watched, enchanted. "They're playing, just like Jeremy and his friends," Jessie exclaimed.

Violet turned back. She saw Winifred Gorman on her deck, working. "I wonder if Ms. Gorman sees them."

"Let's go tell her!" Benny said. He didn't think anybody should miss the dolphins. They all walked back to Winifred Gorman's house.

She saw them coming. "What is it now?" she said grumpily.

"We just wanted to tell you about the dolphins," Violet called out. "They're straight out in front of you. They are so beautiful when they jump like that."

Winifred glanced toward the ocean. "I don't see them."

"We'll come up and show you," said Benny, taking the steps two at a time.

The others followed.

Benny pointed to the spot where the dolphins dove and popped up. "They're the same color as the water, but you'll see them in a minute. There!"

"Now I see them," said Winifred finally, and a faint smile softened her face. "And they *are* beautiful."

Violet was studying the half-finished painting on the easel. It showed another beach scene. "That's very nice," she commented politely.

"No, it isn't." With her brush, Winifred slashed red paint across the canvas. "Listen, you kids, I'm expecting important company."

"We were just going," said Jessie. "Benny wanted to show you the dolphins. That's all."

But Winifred didn't answer or even say good-bye.

When the Aldens were back on the beach, Jessie said, "She never has anything nice to say. What a grouch!"

"She *did* smile a little this time, though," said Violet, and she gazed back at Winifred's deck. "I don't think she's happy with her paintings."

"Well, we can't worry about her," said Henry. "We have to help Officer Hyde find Midnight."

"But first," said Benny, opening the cooler, "I need a soda and some pretzels! I can't think on an empty stomach."

The others laughed.

"You must do a lot of thinking," teased Violet. "Your stomach is never empty, Benny!"

They played catch with a beach ball, then took another dip in the ocean. Soon Jessie spotted Grandfather waving from their deck.

"Time to go in," she told them. "Grandfather warned us not to get sunburned."

They packed up and hopped across the hot sand. When they reached the little boardwalk between Winifred's house and theirs, they set their things down to rinse off with the outdoor hose.

As Henry turned on the water, he noticed a shiny black car in Winifred's driveway.

"Winifred's company is here," he commented.

He handed the hose to Violet and looked at the car. "From New York," he remarked. "The license plate has the Empire State Building on it. Expensive car."

"There he is!" Jessie whispered.

Winifred's guest, a man wearing dark slacks and a white shirt, had just come out on her deck. He sat in a chair at the umbrella table, facing away from the Aldens. Seconds later, Winifred came out, too. She carried two glasses.

"Thanks," said the man. He had a loud voice the Aldens could easily hear. "It's nice here."

"It's different," Winifred said with a shrug. She sat next to him, with her back to the Aldens.

"We should go in," whispered Violet. "They're talking so loud I can hear them without even trying. Is that eavesdropping?"

"We're not eavesdropping," said Jessie. "They're talking extra loud." She and the others began to pick up their belongings.

Just then they heard Winifred ask the man, "What do you think?"

"Well, I could get a good price for the horse in New York," he replied.

Winifred nodded. "The black horse is definitely the best. The others are worthless."

"I'll start lining up a buyer as soon as I get back," the man promised.

The kids stared at one another. They were talking about a black horse! It could only be Midnight.

With his finger to his lips, Henry motioned to them to head inside. They crept down the boardwalk and into the front entrance of Gullwing Cottage.

Once inside, everyone spoke at once.

"She's trying to sell Midnight!" Benny cried.

"We don't know that for sure," said Henry. "But it does sound suspicious. They were definitely talking about a black horse."

"If she took Midnight, where is she keeping him?" asked Violet.

"Even more important," said Jessie direly, "if she somehow managed to capture Midnight, why is she selling him? She could just return him to the herd."

Henry shook his head. "I think Winifred Gorman may have committed a crime."

"Yeah," said Benny. "Horsenapping!"

CHAPTER 6

A Stranger at the Clambake

The children gathered in the living room to discuss what they should do next.

"But how can we prove that Winifred took Midnight?" Violet asked.

"We can't," said Henry. "Not yet, at least. We'll need to look for evidence that Midnight was stolen."

"But we can't let Winifred know that we're suspicious," Jessie pointed out. "We need to act ordinary, like we're on vacation."

"Well, we *are* on vacation!" Benny said with a laugh.

Grandfather came into the room just then.

"We're going to have a clambake for dinner tonight," he said. "Would you like to come with me to the seafood market?"

"Oh, boy!" said Benny, jumping up and down. "A clambake!" Then he stopped hopping. "What's a clambake?"

Everyone laughed.

"You'll see," said Grandfather with a mysterious wink.

The kids changed quickly. Grandfather had promised they could eat lunch out.

The seafood market was located in a group of little stores. The stores were connected by a series of boardwalks along the Sound.

"Can we do some shopping first?" asked Jessie. She had some money saved from her allowance.

"Of course. I'd like to wander around myself," Grandfather said. "Let's meet here in half an hour. Then we can eat at that sandwich place over there."

The four children hurried down the wooden ramp. Henry and Benny went into a shop that sold only games. Jessie and Violet browsed in a jewelry store next door.

"That ring looks good on you," Violet told Jessie, who was trying on a silver dolphin band.

"I think I'll get it," Jessie said, pleased. "What are you buying?"

After much deliberation, Violet chose a dainty chain of silver links.

As the girls were leaving with their purchases, Jessie spotted some odd necklaces on a rack. Dark gray pointed objects dangled from chains.

"These look like teeth!" she remarked.

Violet read the sign. "They are. Ancient sharks' teeth." She shivered. "I don't think I'd want a shark's tooth around my neck!"

Outside, Benny showed them the trick deck of cards he had bought.

Henry had gotten a pocket chess set.

I'm going to teach myself how to play," he said.

They found Grandfather at the sandwich shop. It was crowded, so the Aldens took a number. They sat on high stools along one counter to wait.

Benny twirled on his stool. When it stopped, he was facing a poster on the wall. It showed a picture of a black horse.

"Look," he said, tugging on Jessie's sleeve. "Is that Midnight?"

Jessie scanned the poster. "Yes, it says Midnight is missing."

"I bet these posters are all over the place," said Violet. "Officer Hyde probably had them made."

When their club sandwiches and sodas came, the children filled Grandfather in on the missing stallion.

"I hope Officer Hyde finds him soon," James Alden said.

The children looked at one another. Grandfather didn't know anything about their suspicions. Better to keep it a secret, since Grandfather was hoping for a mystery-free vacation.

After eating, they walked to the seafood market. Grandfather bought a big bucket of clams. Jessie picked out fresh corn, potatoes, and tomatoes.

They returned to the cottage and took the food down to the beach.

Benny was puzzled when he saw the pit Grandfather had dug in the sand earlier in the day.

"Are we going to eat in that hole?" he asked.

Grandfather laughed. "No, the food will steam in this pit. Now I need rocks and wood for a fire."

The girls collected stones and driftwood, while the boys wrapped the potatoes in foil. Then Grandfather laid the rocks in the bottom of the pit. Henry added the driftwood and lit a fire.

"The trick is to let the rocks get hot," said James Alden. "Then we will cover them with wet seaweed."

Henry nodded. "Which makes steam."

"What about the food?" Benny wanted to know. This was certainly a strange way to cook!

"You'll see when the fire burns down and heats the rocks," said Grandfather.

While the fire burned with Grandfather watching over it, Henry, Jessie, Benny, and Violet took a long walk down the beach to collect seaweed. When they returned, the firewood had burned down to a fine ash and the rocks were good and hot. Grandfather carefully laid the weed on the rocks. Then he set the foil-wrapped potatoes on top of the seaweed, then the corn, still in the husk. The clams in their thick shells went on last.

Henry covered the pit with a sheet of heavy canvas and shoveled sand over it to weigh it down.

"Now we can have fun while our dinner cooks," said Grandfather. "It'll be ready in a while."

The afternoon passed quickly. Everyone swam in the ocean, then stretched out under the umbrella to read or nap. Violet drew in her sketchbook.

Jessie was reaching for the sunblock when she saw a figure on the dune. It was a boy with hair so blond it was nearly white. The boy was staring at them. When he saw Jessie sit up, he ducked behind the dune.

Jessie frowned. People here were usually very friendly. And she had the feeling she'd seen him before, but where?

"Food's ready!" Benny called. He and Grandfather were checking under the tarp without lifting it all the way off the steaming mound.

"Not quite yet, Benny," said Grandfather. "But we can bring down plates and drinks."

Jessie and Henry went back to the cottage. She told him about the mysterious boy.

"He was right there," she said, looking up and down the empty dune.

"Well, he's gone now," said Henry.

"I wish I could remember where I'd seen him before," she said.

"It's probably not important," Henry told her. Inside the cottage, he sliced tomatoes while Jessie put silverware, plates, glasses, and napkins into a big basket.

Henry carried the basket down to their blanket on the beach. Jessie followed with a huge thermos of iced tea, a box of chocolate cookies, and a container of butter.

Opening the clambake was exciting. First Henry shoveled off all the sand. Then Grandfather peeled back the heavy canvas. Underneath were sweet, steamed clams, then a layer of juicy corn on the cob, and then the potatoes. The delicious smell of the cooked food filled the air.

They sat cross-legged on the blanket to eat. Jessie finished an ear of corn and as she reached for another she saw the mysterious blond boy peering at them from over the dune's edge again. And again he ducked out of sight when he saw Jessie looking his way.

"This is *delicious!*" Benny exclaimed, licking butter off his fingers.

"It *is* good," agreed Violet with a contented sigh, and they all ate in silence for a while.

Jessie was thinking about the mysterious boy. Suppose he was still nearby, hiding somewhere. It seemed sad, the boy alone while they were all together, happily eating.

While the others were cleaning up, Jessie fixed a plate of leftover clams, corn, tomatoes, and a baked potato. She set the plate on the upturned plastic clam bucket and covered it with another plate. She put a rock on top to hold the plate down.

Then everyone went back to the cottage to take a much-needed shower.

"You should see how much butter and sand you have on you," Violet said to Benny with a giggle.

After they showered, it was still too early to go to bed, so the children asked if they could walk on the beach. Grandfather stayed behind to read the paper.

On the boardwalk, Jessie told the others that she had put out a plate of food just behind the dune for the mysterious boy.

"There's something about that boy," she said. "I know I've seen him somewhere before. I thought he might be hungry, the way he was staring at our clambake."

"He might have been just curious," said Henry. "But it was a good idea, Jessie."

Thick gray mist rolled in from the ocean. Tatters of fog blew across the dune like ghostly flags.

Through the mist Jessie spied a figure walking down the beach ahead of them. The person was carrying a bucket.

"I bet that's him!" she exclaimed. "He's carrying the bucket I put the plate on."

Violet stared into the fog. "I can't tell if it's a boy or not. And the bucket looks heavy, the way he's carrying it. What could be in it?"

Beside her, Benny froze.

"What is it?" she asked him.

A break in the wispy clouds unveiled a silvery moon. Bathed in moonlight, a horse galloped across the sand. Puffs of sand shot up from its hoofs.

The horse pelted down the beach, well beyond the figure with the bucket.

"It's Magic, the ghost horse!" Benny cried.

And then the horse was gone, vanished like a breath in the mist.

"I just had a glimpse," said Henry. "Too foggy to tell what color it was."

"Let's follow him," Benny suggested. "Maybe we can catch him!"

Ragged clouds closed over the moon, shutting out the light. Like ghostly smoke, fog blanketed the beach.

"The fog is even heavier now," Henry said. "It's too dangerous. We have to go back."

Jessie shivered. What had they just seen?

The next morning was clear, with no sign of fog. After a quick breakfast, the Alden children hurried to the beach.

"I put the bucket right here," said Jessie. "It's gone! So is my plate of food."

"The person we saw last night was walking up here," said Henry. Soon he found a line of prints. He put his own foot next to one. "A little bigger than mine."

"It could be an older boy," said Jessie. "Like Jeremy or one of his friends."

"Those prints could also belong to a woman," Violet pointed out. "Like Winifred. We're in front of her house."

"Shad's feet aren't very big, either," Benny added. "Let's see if we can find hoofprints."

But last night's tide had washed the shoreline clean.

"We definitely saw a horse," said Jessie. "We couldn't have *all* been dreaming."

"But who was the person?" Violet asked.

"Let's go visit Winifred," suggested Henry. "We can ask her if she was out walking last night. And we can look at the size of her shoe at the same time."

For once, Winifred Gorman seemed to be waiting for the Aldens. She was standing in her carport, hands on her hips.

"There you are!" she said, her face angry under the straw hat. "I have a bone to pick with you kids!"

CHAPTER 7

The Shark's Tooth Necklace

"What are you talking about?" Jessie asked.

Winifred glared at them. "I left a bowl of apples here yesterday. I'd just bought them so I could paint a still life today. Now they're gone!"

"You think we took your apples?" said Henry. "Why would we do that?"

"I don't know," said Winifred, holding up the empty bowl. "Things keep disappearing around here."

"Well, we're not doing it," Benny said

defensively. Then he added, "But we saw somebody on the beach last night. He was carrying a bucket — "

" — and the bucket looked heavy," Violet broke in. "Like it could have had apples in it."

"Did you see who this person was?" Winifred demanded.

Jessie shook her head. "No. We were wondering if you noticed anybody walking past your place. It was around nine o'clock."

"I was watching the news then." Winifred set the bowl down. "I'll have to paint something else, I guess."

Abruptly she went inside her house.

Jessie clucked her tongue. "That woman has the worst manners! She doesn't even say good-bye, after she accused us of stealing her apples."

"She's not very polite," Henry agreed. "But at least we found out one thing. She was in her house when we saw that person, so it couldn't have been her."

"That's what she *says*," Benny replied. He wasn't sure he trusted the artist.

"I looked at her feet," Violet reported. She held her hands apart. "They're *really* big."

Jessie giggled. "Yeah! Way bigger than the footprints we found."

"Okay," said Henry. "So it wasn't Winifred who left those prints."

The children wandered down to the beach again. They walked along the water's edge and discussed the case.

"Who keeps taking Winifred's stuff?" asked Jessie.

"My stuff, too," Benny said. "Somebody swiped my peanut butter, banana, and mayonnaise sandwich, remember?"

Violet ticked off the missing items on one hand. "Winifred's beach towel, Benny's sandwich, and now the apples. Things taken from our house and her house."

"But not Jeremy's house," Henry observed, glancing back at the brown house. "The college kids haven't complained once about anything being stolen."

Violet thought of something. "The person we saw last night was walking toward the college kids' house — "

"And Jeremy likes to play jokes," Henry reminded them. "He told us so himself. Suppose he took the towel and the apples to be funny. And remember how he 'borrowed' a goat to play a joke on his professor?"

"I suppose he could be a suspect," Jessie admitted reluctantly. She thought Jeremy was nice.

Violet stooped to pick up a rosy shell. "Who else can we think of?"

"In which case?" asked Henry.

"What do you mean?" Violet said.

Henry tossed a pebble into a tide pool. "We've got two mysteries here. The missing items. And the missing horse."

"Midnight is more important than a bunch of apples," Benny declared. "What could have happened to him?"

"Well, we saw the picture Winifred painted of a black horse," said Jessie. "I bet that horse is Midnight."

"But she claimed she didn't see any horses the day she drove to the sanctuary," Violet said.

"Like Benny said, that's what she *told* us," said Henry. "Maybe she got Midnight away from the herd, took him somewhere, and painted his picture."

"Or maybe she isn't only an artist but also a horse thief," said Violet. "Maybe she paints a horse and finds a buyer by showing the painting."

"I don't know," said Henry. "She said she'd moved here without really knowing anything about the horses."

"But maybe she told us that on purpose!" Jessie said.

Henry looked at his sisters with approval. "Those are interesting theories. You two got a lot out of that conversation we overheard."

Jessie and Violet smiled at each other.

"What do you think Winifred meant when she said the horse was 'the best' and the others were 'worthless'?" Violet wanted to know.

Jessie thought a moment. "Maybe when she saw the herd she figured Midnight was the prettiest and that's why she painted him. The others aren't as pretty."

"I think they are," Benny chimed in.

"I think so, too," said Violet. "But Winifred is an artist. She sees things in a different way."

"We can't rule out Jeremy, either," Henry said. "He keeps talking about the big stunts he pulled. If he took Midnight, that would be a *really* big stunt."

"You're right," agreed Benny. "Jeremy could have horsenapped Midnight as easily as Winifred."

"We're forgetting a suspect," said Violet. "Shad."

Henry nodded. "Shad has the biggest reason of all for taking Midnight."

"What's that?" asked Benny. He liked the old fisherman.

"He hates the way the ponies are locked up," Henry replied. "Shad wants them loose, like they used to be."

Jessie threw up her hands. "As usual, we have a lot of questions and no answers!

Let's check where I put the food out last night. Maybe we'll find a clue we over-looked."

Near the dune, they located a ring-shaped mark in the sand where the bucket had stood.

Benny noticed a glint of silver tangled in the sea grass. He pulled out a fine silver chain with a dark gray object dangling from it.

"What is *this*?" he asked, holding up the chain.

Jessie knew instantly. "It's a shark's tooth. Violet and I saw necklaces just like that in the jewelry store yesterday."

"A real shark's tooth?" Benny was fascinated.

"Whoever took your food probably lost this necklace at the same time," Henry said to Jessie. "Probably when he — or she — bent over."

"Can I have it?" Benny asked. The necklace was the coolest thing he'd ever seen.

"We might find the owner," Jessie told him. "So I'd better hang on to it for safekeeping. But the next time we go to those little shops, Violet and I will buy you a shark's tooth."

As he watched his sister stow the necklace in her shorts pocket, Benny had a niggling thought. The necklace looked sort of familiar.

Where had he seen a necklace like that before?

Shad was fishing at the end of the dock, sitting on an old camp stool. The brown pelican eyed Shad's bait in a plastic fish-market bucket.

Jessie realized the bucket was just like the one their clams had come in. Was it the same bucket? Was it Shad who took the plate of food she'd put out last night?

"Mornin'," he greeted them.

"Hi," said Henry. "Catch anything yet?"

"A few minnows," Shad replied. "Threw 'em back. What are y'all doing up so early?"

"We were walking on the beach," said Violet.

Jessie pulled the necklace out of her

pocket. "We found this. We wondered if it might be yours." If the necklace belonged to Shad, then she'd know he had taken the food plate.

Shad shook his head. "Not mine. Nobody I know wears one of those. You know, it's bad luck to wear them."

"Really?" Benny's eyes grew round.

"Well . . . that's what I've heard." Suddenly Shad became very interested in checking his line.

Jessie was certain he was making that up, about shark's teeth being bad luck. But why?

The older man rose. "I just remembered. I have to go home." Reeling in his line, he picked up his rod and bucket and clumped down the dock.

"That was weird," said Violet. "He didn't want to talk to us this time."

"He's certainly acting suspicious," said Henry. "I wonder if he catches all his food. He's always fishing, either on this dock or on the beach."

"He must get sick of fish," said Benny, who didn't much like fish himself.

Jessie agreed. "He's kind of thin. I wonder if he's hungry." Then she thought, Was Shad so hungry he had to steal food?

At that moment, the kids heard a piercing whistle.

"What's that?" asked Violet.

"It's coming from the road," said Benny. "Let's check it out."

They ran down the dock and across the short, cropped grass by the road.

Thomas Hyde was standing in the middle of the two-lane road. He was halting traffic by blowing a whistle and holding up his hands.

When the cars had stopped, several ponies poked their heads through the bayberry bushes.

"Look!" cried Benny. "They're coming over to our side!"

The horses daintily stepped onto the road and crossed single file. Tourists in their cars clapped at the sight. A few snapped pictures. Violet wished she had brought her own camera.

When the horses were safely on the other side, Officer Hyde dropped his hands and gave a short all-clear blast on his whistle. Traffic moved once more.

The kids watched as the horses nibbled grass on the bank. Officer Hyde joined them.

"Good morning," he said. "You guys are really lucky. Tourists wait all summer to see the horses away from the sanctuary. Most people never *do* see them."

"We've seen them three times," Benny said. "Twice at the sanctuary and now here. Will they be all right?"

"I'll stay with them," Officer Hyde said. "Eventually I'll get them back to the pen. They like to roam. It's only natural. At one time, the whole island was theirs. Now they have to stay in one little corner of it."

"Did you find Midnight?" Henry asked.

Officer Hyde shook his head. "But I'll tell you what I did find. A break in the dune fence on the Sound side. Black hair was snagged on a broken slat."

"Is Midnight hurt?" asked Violet, concerned.

"He could be," Officer Hyde replied. "That was obviously where Midnight escaped — or was forced — from the sanctuary. If he's hurt, he probably needs medical attention."

The Aldens looked at one another.

Midnight must be found . . . and fast!

CHAPTER 8

What Shad Knows

"Let's have our lunch on the deck," Jessie suggested.

"Good idea." Henry loaded a tray with egg-salad sandwiches and a plate of carrot and celery sticks.

Violet followed him out the sliding glass doors with a pitcher of limeade.

The children sat down on the deck chairs and began eating.

Jessie was looking at Winifred Gorman's house. The artist had come out on her own deck. She saw the Alden children and waved.

"Come on over," she called. "I made brownies."

Jessie looked at Henry in astonishment. "Did she just invite us over for brownies?"

"You heard right," he said, raising his eyebrows. "Let's go. It'll be a good chance to find out more about the pony painting."

Violet stacked their lunch things on the tray. "I'll be right out. I want to show something to Winifred."

She returned moments later with her sketch pad. Then the kids walked over to their neighbor's house.

Winifred had arranged the chairs around the umbrella table. A plate of vanilla-iced brownies sat in the middle.

"Help yourself," she said. "If you don't, I'll eat them all myself. My waistline can't afford it!"

Benny was confused. First Winifred was mad at them. She thought they had stolen her apples. Now she was giving them brownies. But Benny couldn't resist. He took a brownie and tasted it. He never turned down chocolate.

"Mmm," he pronounced. "Good."

Winifred smiled. Benny had never seen the woman smile before. Why was she so nice all of a sudden?

"May I show you something?" Violet asked the artist. "It's a drawing I did."

"Sure!" Winifred opened Violet's book and examined the sketch of a bird. "You used one line! Isn't that a fun technique?"

"Did I do it right?" Violet asked anxiously.

"Art is about expressing oneself," said Winifred. "There is no right or wrong way."

"Can you draw like that? Just using one line?" Violet wanted to know.

"Of course." Winifred reached down by her chair for her own drawing pad. Taking a pencil from her pocket, she flipped to a fresh page. "You can draw people this way, too. Just put your pencil down and start with the eyes — don't pick up your pencil until you're done."

As she talked, she rapidly sketched Violet's features using a single line. She tore off the page and gave it to Violet.

Violet was thrilled. "That's wonderful! Thank you."

As Winifred closed her sketchbook, Henry noticed a drawing of another face. The artist saw him looking and closed the book quickly.

Henry was suspicious. Why had Winifred invited them over? She usually acted like they were a nuisance. The woman must want something from them, but what? Maybe if he learned more about her . . .

"Are you going to live here all the time?" he asked.

"I have a studio in New York City," said Winifred. "This summer I came down here on vacation."

"Like us," Benny put in.

Winifred smiled. "Well, I took a vacation from my work. People aren't buying my paintings. I thought a change of scenery would be good for me."

"And has it been?" asked Jessie.

"I think it has," the artist replied. "I might sell my studio and live here all the time. It's very peaceful."

"Except for the robberies," Henry brought up.

Winifred frowned. "What robberies?"

"You know, your missing beach towel. And the apples."

"Oh, those," Winifred said. "I found the beach towel the other day. As for the apples, no great loss."

"But you were really upset," Benny reminded her.

"That's because I was worried about my work," she explained. "I know I haven't been a very nice neighbor, and I'm sorry about that," she added quietly. "But now I'm painting better than ever. A bowl of missing apples is nothing."

Jessie was amazed at how Winifred had changed her tune. Every time they had seen the woman, she was grouchy. Now she was nice as pie! What was going on?

At that moment, Benny stood up. "Grandfather's back," he said. Then he saw another car pull into the driveway behind their station wagon.

The car had a star painted on the side. It was from the sheriff's office.

By the time the children ran over to the cottage, two uniformed deputies were sitting in the living room with Grandfather.

"I'm Deputy Knight," said a tall, dark-haired man with a deep tan. "And this is Deputy Perelli." His brown-haired companion nodded.

"I'm James Alden," said Grandfather. "These are my grandchildren, Henry, Jessie, Violet, and Benny. How may we help you?"

Deputy Knight removed a black-and-white photograph from his clipboard and passed it to Grandfather.

"Have you seen this boy? We think he is somewhere in the vicinity," said the officer.

James Alden studied the photograph, then shook his head before handing it to Henry. "No, I'm sorry. I've never seen him."

The others gathered around Henry. The photograph showed a blond-haired boy

around fifteen years old. He was wearing a necklace.

Benny was startled. He was sure he'd seen that boy's picture before. It was in the newspaper Grandfather had bought their first day. But the boy wasn't by himself. He was in a group of other boys.

Jessie thought she recognized that face, but she wasn't sure. It looked like the blond boy she'd seen watching them from the dune yesterday. And the boy she'd spied carrying the Seagull Resort beach chair.

"Who is this boy?" Grandfather asked the deputies.

"His name is Austin Derrick," Deputy Perelli replied. "He has run away from summer camp on the mainland. We have reason to believe he is hiding on the island."

Deputy Knight continued the explanation. "Apparently Austin didn't want to go to this camp. He argued with his parents, but they both had long business trips this summer. Austin went to camp, but left after the first week."

"Did he call his parents?" Grandfather asked, concerned.

"Yes, he did," said Deputy Perelli. "He told them he was with a friend. But they checked out his story. The friend he was supposed to be staying with hasn't seen Austin all summer. So then they called the police. The parents are on their way now. They should be here by this evening."

"Why do they think he is here?" Grandfather probed.

"Because the boy's father has an older, distant cousin who lives here," replied Deputy Knight. "Apparently Austin spent a few summers with the cousin. He was angry when he learned he couldn't stay with the relative this summer."

Grandfather nodded sympathetically. "Sounds like the boy is lonely, with his parents away a lot. Have you contacted the cousin yet?"

"He doesn't have a phone," said Deputy Knight. "And we can't locate him at his residence. We'll keep trying, but we're worried because his house is quite a bit out of the way, and it's possible that the boy may have become lost. That's why we're checking out the whole island."

"We'd like to help," said Grandfather. "My grandchildren and I will keep an eye out for this boy. We'll call you if we see him."

The officers stood and shook Grandfather's hand.

"Thanks for your cooperation," said Deputy Perelli.

As Grandfather showed the men to the door, Benny went over to the coffee table. He found the old newspaper, tore a page from it, folded it, and jammed it into his pocket.

Henry watched his brother and knew Benny was on to something.

"We're going out," said Henry to Grandfather. "We need some air."

Outside, they all began talking at once.

Henry held up a silencing hand. "Wait a minute! I know Benny knows something."

"So does Jessie," said Violet. "She's got that look on her face. Spill, you two."

Benny and Jessie told Violet and Henry where they thought they had seen the boy before. Benny showed them the newspaper photograph of the campers. Sure enough, the blond boy stood in the front row.

Violet gasped. "It *is* him! You can even see the shark's tooth necklace around his neck!"

"I knew I'd seen that necklace someplace else before. But who could the relative be the policemen were talking about?" Benny wondered out loud.

"I have an idea," said Henry. "Follow me."

He led them across the road to the docks. At the end of the dock, Shad Toler was cleaning his catch. Shad's pelican friend was watching intently.

The fisherman looked up when he saw them approach.

"Hey," he said. "Think I ought to throw Greedy here a fish?"

Henry glanced into the bucket. Shad had caught a lot of fish today — enough to feed two people.

"I don't know if you can spare a fish," he

said carefully. "It depends on how much Austin eats."

Shad stared at him. "Pardon?"

Benny showed him the newspaper photo. "Some policemen came to our house today. They're looking for this boy. Do you know him?"

"What makes you think I'd know him?" Shad said, suddenly unable to look them in the eye.

Jessie pulled the shark's tooth necklace from her pocket. "This is Austin Derrick's necklace. We found it on the beach. When we showed it to you, you said it was bad luck to wear shark's teeth. But I think you were really afraid that we'd find out about Austin."

Violet noticed the sky behind them growing very dark. A storm was approaching from the mainland. She remembered what Grandfather had said about storms being dangerous on the Outer Banks.

"Storm's comin'," Shad said nervously. "I've got to go home and . . . check on things."

"Maybe we should come with you," said Henry. "I think it's time we found out the whole story."

Shad looked out over the water. "Maybe it *is* time you knew. I'm getting tired of keeping secrets."

CHAPTER 9

SOS

Shad walked the Aldens to his place. It seemed to take a long time and the sky grew darker all the while. He lived in an old house with several outbuildings near the shore.

"Come see this first," said Shad, leading them to a shack half buried in a thicket of wild grapevines.

Rusty crab pots and ripped fishing nets hung from plank walls. In the middle of the floor was a narrow, low platform covered with a bright green beach towel. Nearby was a fish-market bucket half filled with apples. The only other furniture was a blue canvas beach chair.

"That looks like our bucket," Jessie said. "And those must be Winifred Gorman's apples. And her beach towel. I wonder why she said she found it."

"I bet that chair belongs to the Seagull Resort," Violet added. "It has the same seagull design on it."

Henry looked at Shad. "Is this Austin's hideout?"

Shad nodded ruefully. "I didn't know he was here until a few days ago. He told me his folks dropped him off, which I thought was strange. All he had was his backpack. This morning when I was doing chores, I found this shack had been fixed up. He's been here longer than I thought."

"You didn't know Austin had run away?" said Benny.

Shad shook his head. "Something seemed funny, the way he just showed up. But his parents are always traveling, so it seemed possible they would leave him with me for a while. He's always welcome here. I supposed they could have been in a big hurry and didn't have time to talk to me. But, like I said, it's strange."

"His parents called the police," Henry said.

"When you told me the police were looking for him, I figured Austin was in trouble," said Shad. "He hid out in this old fishing shack until he got too hungry. Then he came to me. Told me that story about his parents dropping him off. I think he's scared, too."

"We can help him," said Jessie. "Where is he?"

"Up at my place." Shad pointed toward a rambling wooden house at the end of a sandy driveway.

As they walked to Shad's house, Henry noticed an old Cadillac convertible parked in the yard.

"Cool car," he said.

"Hasn't run in years," Shad informed him. "But I get by without one. I walk anyplace I need to go."

Violet glanced back at the threatening sky. "We'd better hurry inside."

They thudded up on the porch. Shad opened the front door, which was unlocked.

His house was plainly furnished with an old sofa, scuffed coffee table, and a well-used rocking chair. In the kitchen was an oak dining table with four matching chairs. A carved duck decoy stood on the fireplace mantel.

There was no sign of Austin Derrick other than a burgundy backpack lying in the corner.

"Austin!" Shad called into the two small bedrooms and single bathroom. "Where are you, boy?"

Henry watched gray storm clouds gather outside. Wind whipped the trees as thunder rumbled over the sea.

Shad came back, his face creased with worry. "He's not here!"

"Where could he be?" Violet asked.

"I don't know," said Shad. "Unless . . ."

"Unless what?" Henry demanded. "You have to tell us everything or we can't help."

At that moment, a clap of thunder rattled the windowpanes. Shad switched on the lights.

Violet ran to look out. "It's starting to rain. If Austin isn't under cover, he'll get soaked."

Before she finished speaking, rain fell from the sky in sheets. It was impossible to see out the windows. Seconds later, the refrigerator in the kitchen quit humming and the lights blinked off.

"Power's out," Shad declared. "Happens a lot on the Banks. Wait just a minute."

He fumbled in a side table drawer, pulling out candles and a box of matches. He also drew out a large flashlight, which he clicked on briefly to test the batteries.

"Should have bought batteries this week," he muttered.

Jessie helped him light the candles. The flickering flames made the old house seem spooky, especially with the trees lashing outside.

"I hear something!" said Benny. "It sounds like . . . a horse. I bet it's Magic!"

Shad looked at him. "Do you really hear a horse? Your ears are sharper than mine."

Henry heard the noise, too. "It's not an animal. It's a person!"

Heavy footsteps clumped on the porch. Then the front door burst open.

A very wet blond boy stood in the doorway.

Shad ran over to him. "Where have you been?"

"I've been checking on — " Just then Austin saw the Aldens and broke off. He looked as if he might run outside again. "Who are they?" he asked, instantly suspicious.

"They're okay," Shad reassured him.

Violet found Shad's bathroom and brought Austin a towel.

"The police are looking for you," Shad told Austin.

"Your parents are very worried," added Henry. "They thought you might be here, but no one could find Shad."

"I don't have a phone," Shad said. "And I'm out all day."

"I knew this was a mistake," Austin moaned.

"Why did you run away?" asked Benny.

Austin looked miserable, dripping on the bare floor. "I didn't want to go to camp," he replied. "My folks are always gone. I wanted them to stay home with me. They said they couldn't, so I asked if I could visit Shad."

"And they wouldn't let you?" asked Violet.

Austin shook his head. "They'd already signed me up for camp. Camp was okay, but I wanted to be with Shad. So I called my folks at their hotel and told them I was staying with a kid I know. Then I left."

"How did you get here?" Henry asked.

"The camp is over on the mainland," Austin replied. "Just over the bridge. I got a ride with the guy who delivers bread to the camp. He lives over here. I told him I was spending the weekend with another kid in Southern Shores. He let me out there and I walked the rest of the way."

Benny was amazed. "You sure like to make up stuff!"

Austin looked sheepish. "I guess I do. My mom says I let my imagination run away with me."

"That's not all that ran away," Shad said sternly. "You shouldn't have left that camp without your folks' permission."

"I knew you'd say that," Austin told Shad. "That's why I hid in your fishing shack the first few days."

"I can't believe I never even knew you were there," said Shad.

Jessie remembered the scene at the restaurant. "Did you try to get a job as a busboy at the Seagull Resort?"

Austin nodded. "How did you know?"

"We were there the night the waiter got mad because you dropped the tray," she replied.

"I needed money for food," said Austin. "I was willing to work for it, but nobody would give me a job. So I had to — " Once more, he broke off and flushed with embarrassment.

"Steal," Violet finished for him. "You took Benny's sandwich from our deck."

"Was that your sandwich?" Austin asked Benny. "Sorry."

"I'm sorry you were hungry," said Benny.

At that moment, thunder crashed and the door was flung open. Winifred Gorman clung to the door frame, drenched.

Austin ran over to her. "Did you find him?" he asked.

"Yes," she reported, taking off her wet hat. "He's on the other side of the ravine. I can't get him out. We need help."

Shad's jaw tightened. "Austin, if anything happens to him . . ."

Jessie was confused. "Do you all know one another?" she asked Austin.

"Winnie and I just met a couple of days ago," he replied. "And Shad met Winnie today."

Winnie! Jessie couldn't believe her ears. Their grumpy neighbor was friends with a runaway boy!

"What are you kids doing here?" asked Winifred as Violet handed her a towel.

"We came to help Austin," Henry answered. "It sounds like someone else needs help, too. And I bet I know who — or should I say what? — it is."

Violet caught on instantly. "Midnight! You have Midnight!"

"You're the horsenapper!" Benny accused Austin.

"It's a long story and I don't have time to tell it now," said Austin. "Midnight is in danger. The storm must be making him wild with fear."

Shad turned to the Aldens. "Remember when I told you about the ravine?" he said. "Years ago a big storm cut a channel through my land. When we have a lot of rain, the ravine fills with water."

"Midnight is stranded on a small rise between the water-filled ravine and the sea," said Winifred. "He might be a good swimmer, but the storm frightened him. Also, his leg isn't that strong. If he is panicked by the lightning and tries to swim, he may drown."

"Midnight is hurt?" queried Benny.

Austin nodded. "He can walk and run, but I don't think he can jump over the ravine. He might fall in. We've got to calm him down and walk him the long way around. I can't manage it alone."

Jessie looked at Henry. "We're wasting time talking," she said. "We need to get help, fast."

"No phone," Shad reminded her. "Car doesn't run and we're way off the road. How are we going to get help in a hurry?"

Jessie remembered that night at the restaurant. Seeing Shad waving his flashlight gave her an idea.

"Your flashlight! We can use it to signal SOS." Then she bit her lip. "Only I don't know what the signal *is*!"

"I do," said Henry, taking the flashlight. "It's Morse code. You can use the same code with light."

Everyone rushed outside. Winifred stayed on the porch and the rest ran to a clearing well away from trees.

"Which way is the road?" Henry yelled above the thrashing storm.

Shad pointed. "Over there. Will the beam be strong enough to shine through this rain?"

"All we can do is try. The storm clouds have darkened the sky so much, it's almost like night." Henry aimed the flashlight and pressed the button. He sent three short flashes of light, followed by three long flashes, then three more short flashes.

"Do it again," instructed Jessie. "We'll probably have to signal several times to get anyone's attention."

Henry flashed the light over and over, three shorts, three longs, three shorts.

"Uh-oh," he said, shaking the flashlight. "The battery must be getting weak."

The beam was growing dimmer. How long before the flashlight would be dead? Henry wondered.

Just then, a bolt of lightning cut the sky.

Benny gulped. The white-hot lightning was in the shape of a horse's head!

Was it Magic come back to help them?

Seconds later, a car horn blared. *Beep! Beep! Beep! Beep!*

Then a figure swathed in rain gear strode into the clearing.

CHAPTER 10

Benny's Promise

Benny recognized the figure instantly.

"Officer Hyde!" he exclaimed, running to meet him. "Midnight is in trouble!"

Thomas Hyde looked sternly at everyone. "What's going on? Where is Midnight?"

"On the other side of the ravine," said Jessie. "It's filled with water. Midnight is too scared to jump across."

"Who knows where he is?" Officer Hyde demanded.

"I do," replied Austin.

"How deep is this ravine?" asked Officer Hyde.

"Pretty deep," Shad replied. "The horse could jump across, but he's got a hurt leg, and we're afraid he'd drown."

"Take me to him now," Officer Hyde ordered Austin. "And I'll need someone else to help." His eye fell on Henry. "Henry, you come with us."

From his Jeep, Officer Hyde retrieved extra flashlights, ponchos for the boys, and a sturdy rope.

"Can we come, too?" asked Violet.

Officer Hyde shook his head. "Too many people will make Midnight skittish. We will get as close as we can with the Jeep. Midnight is wild, but he knows me. I think if the three of us stay calm and move slowly, he will let me put a rope around his neck and we can lead him to safety. We'll be back as soon as we can."

Everyone was too anxious to go back inside, so they waited on Shad's porch.

"I hope Midnight is okay," said Benny.

"I told Austin it was a fool thing to keep that animal," Shad muttered. "And I'd made him promise to call the sanctuary tomorrow, to let them know he'd found him."

Jessie stared at Shad. "You knew about the horse?"

"Not until the other day," Shad replied. "I found tracks by my old barn. Austin told me he had found the horse loose and hurt. He decided to befriend him."

"Where was Austin going to keep him?" asked Benny. "It's kind of hard to hide a horse."

"It sure is!" Shad agreed. "But I've got a fair piece of property and it's all fenced in. Nobody comes snooping around here. Well, not most people, anyway," he added, and he shot Winifred a glance.

They stood and waited on the porch, watching the rain for what seemed like a long time. No one had the heart to go on talking. They were all worried about Midnight. Then they saw movement in the weeds of Shad's yard.

"Here they come!" Winifred exclaimed.

Henry, Austin, and Thomas Hyde came into view. Soaked to the skin, they tromped up onto the porch.

"We got him around," Thomas reported. "Midnight is in your old barn, Shad."

"He'll be safe there," Shad said. "Till you move him up to the sanctuary."

"I'll drive you Aldens back to your cottage so you can get out of those wet things," said Officer Hyde. "Ms. Gorman, too."

Shad nodded. "Austin's folks ought to arrive sometime tomorrow, unless they are delayed by the storm."

"Shad!" Austin exclaimed. "You called my parents?"

"Yes," said Shad. "I just didn't feel right about them not knowing where you really were. I called them from the public phone at the docks. I planned to tell you before they arrived."

"Bring Austin back to my place for now," Winifred offered. "The phones might still be working there. And I have a coffeemaker that works without electricity."

Everyone but Shad climbed into Officer Hyde's Jeep. When they arrived at Gullwing Cottage, Grandfather met them at the door. He looked anxious.

"I've been worried," he said. "You got caught in the storm. The power went off for a while — "

"They're all fine," Officer Hyde reassured him. "Just very wet."

"We found Midnight!" Benny crowed. "He's been hiding at Shad's! Austin took him."

Grandfather looked puzzled.

"It's a long story," said Officer Hyde. "Go change, kids, and we'll meet at Ms. Gorman's house."

The children quickly put on dry clothes. By the time they left the cottage, it had stopped raining and the sun was setting behind the receding storm clouds.

Winifred cheerfully introduced herself to Grandfather as she invited them all inside.

Violet loved Winifred's house. The walls were decorated with colorful paintings. Funny sculptures sat on the white wicker tables. And the painting of a black horse — obviously Midnight — was prominently displayed on an easel.

Winifred had changed and was wearing a long, loose, silky blue dress. Green pottery mugs waited on a round wooden tray, along with a plate of butter cookies.

"The coffee will be just a minute," she said. "I have juice for you young people."

"Do Austin's parents know where he is?" asked Grandfather.

"Yes, Shad called them earlier today." She scooped coffee grounds into a glass beaker, then poured in boiling water. "It seems they're still on the mainland because of the storm. But Officer Hyde says they've talked to the sheriff's office here and the search for Austin has been called off."

When everyone had been served, they sat around the large glass table.

"Austin, you know running away and taking Midnight are both serious offenses," said Officer Hyde.

Austin nodded, swallowing. "I knew it was wrong. But I wasn't going to keep him.

And I know I shouldn't have run away in the first place."

"But why didn't you go to Shad's right away?" said Henry.

"I was afraid he'd make me tell my folks and I'd have to go back to camp," Austin replied.

"I did, finally!" Shad said emphatically.

"So that's why I hid out," Austin continued. "It was okay at first. I walked all over the island. One evening I found Midnight. He was limping. He had a scrape on his front leg. So I took him back to Shad's barn."

"Didn't you know it's against the law to touch the wild horses, much less *take* one?" asked Thomas Hyde.

"I didn't really *take* him. I *found* him. I don't know much about those rules, but I could see the horse was like me: lonely. I wanted to help him. So I washed his leg and tore up my T-shirt to make a bandage."

"I discovered the horse," Shad admitted. "I knew Austin had done wrong, but I felt sorry for both of them: the horse shut away, the boy sent away. So I put some medicine on Midnight's leg, bandaged it right. I knew we couldn't keep that horse hidden for long. Austin promised he'd call the sanctuary tomorrow."

"You told us about Magic to confuse us," accused Jessie. "In case we ever saw a horse, we'd think it was the ghost horse."

"So you *wanted* me to think the horse I saw was a ghost?" Benny asked.

"I'm not proud of that story I told you," said Shad. "I did have a reason. One night Midnight got out. Austin went after him. The horse was loose on the beach. Austin called, trying to get him back."

"That was the cry I heard," Benny concluded. "But the horse wasn't Magic?"

Henry shook his head. "No, Benny."

"I finally caught him way down the beach," Austin said. "And got him back in Shad's barn. The next day, Shad found him."

Henry nodded. "That explains why we couldn't find your footprints. We didn't walk far enough."

Grandfather had been studying the horse painting. "You painted Midnight," he said to Winifred. "You knew about the missing horse, too."

"Not at first," said Winifred. "I actually saw Midnight before I knew anything about a missing horse. I could hardly believe my eyes. I'd been having trouble sleeping and got up to look out the back door and there he was, looking glorious on the dunes. He was gone in a moment. I almost thought I'd dreamed him. I sketched him immediately. In the morning, before the sun was up, I'd finished the painting. I know I told you I hadn't seen a horse, but I never like to talk about my paintings and I almost wanted to believe he had been a dream. *My* dream." Winifred looked at the children. "I'm sorry I lied to you."

Austin spoke up. "Winnie's cool. I took some apples from her carport one night. Midnight likes apples." He turned to Jessie. "I found the plate of food you put out from your clambake. Thanks."

Jessie nodded. "I saw you earlier. I thought you might be hungry."

"We saw someone carrying a heavy bucket," Violet said to Austin. "That was you, taking Winifred's apples."

"The foggy night," Henry remembered. "We saw a phantom horse, like Magic."

"It was Midnight," Austin said. "He got out again. I lured him back to Shad's with the apples."

"How do you fit in?" Grandfather asked Winifred.

She spread her hands, indicating her paintings on the walls. "My art had not been going well. I came here to see if my work would improve. Violet saw one of my paintings and suggested I add animals. After I saw and painted Midnight, I was thrilled. I wanted to paint him again."

"We thought *you* had taken Midnight," said Benny. "And you were going to sell him to that New York man."

Winifred laughed. "That New York man is my agent! He sells my paintings!"

"We heard you say the black horse was

the best," Violet explained. "And that the others were worthless. Then the man said he'd get a good price for the horse in New York. We thought you were talking about the island's horses."

"You only heard part of it," Winifred said. "I meant the horse painting was the best — the rest of my *work* was worthless. My agent said he'd get a good price for the horse painting in New York."

"I met Winnie yesterday," said Austin. "I was out looking for my necklace when I saw her on her deck sketching. I couldn't help but notice that the horse she was drawing looked like Midnight. Then she took her charcoal and darkened the horse and I was sure it was Midnight. It was so beautiful I had to say something — even though I didn't want anyone to know about Midnight — or me. Winnie told me she'd glimpsed the horse only once — that she wasn't even sure he was real and that she'd been to the sanctuary several times hoping to see him again. She seemed to care for him as much as I did, and after she promised she would keep my secret, I took her to see him."

Winifred was smiling warmly at Austin.

"Then I told her I took her beach towel and her apples and she said she didn't care anymore. She even drew my picture."

"And we hit it off, didn't we, Austin? You, Midnight, and I," Winifred said.

Officer Hyde put his empty mug on the table. "Well, I must get back to the herd. Midnight will be fine in Shad's barn till tomorrow. Then I'm taking him back to the sanctuary." He looked sternly at Austin. "I'll also talk to the sheriff and discuss your keeping Midnight at Shad's, Austin."

Austin stared at the floor.

"Austin is going home with me tonight," said Shad. "His folks will be at my place in about an hour."

"How about if we all meet tomorrow morning at the sanctuary?" said Officer Hyde, going to the door. "I'm sure everyone wants to see Midnight returned safely."

"We'll be there," Grandfather said to Winifred. "We should going, too. Thanks for the coffee."

Benny looked back at Austin. The boy's shoulders were slumped in misery.

What would happen to him?

The next morning the sky was blue, as if the storm had scrubbed it extra-clean.

The Aldens and Winifred left early for the sanctuary.

A crowd gathered at the sanctuary gate — the Aldens, Winifred, Officer Hyde, and Shad. Austin introduced his parents, Mr. and Mrs. Derrick, to everyone. They had arrived the night before and seemed very glad to be with their son. Officer Hyde had brought Midnight from Shad's in a horse trailer.

He backed the trailer into the open gate and let down the ramp. Midnight walked off and immediately joined several members of the herd who had climbed over the dune out of curiosity.

"I promised we'd find Midnight!" Benny called to the horses.

"Will he be the leader again?" Violet wanted to know.

Officer Hyde nodded. "I think it'll be all right."

"What about me?" Austin asked nervously.

"I've discussed the case with the sheriff and the sheriff has spoken with our local judge," said Officer Hyde. "Since you are underage, we decided you have to pay the fine for taking Midnight, but instead of a sentence, you will do community service."

"But Austin doesn't live here," said Mrs. Derrick.

"He can stay with me, if that is all right with his parents and the authorities," said Shad.

"And I would like to help pay the fine," offered Winifred.

"That's quite all right — " Mr. Derrick began.

"Please let me," said Winifred. "I knew about the horse and should have told the authorities immediately."

"What kind of community service will I be doing?" Austin asked Officer Hyde.

"Working with the horses," he answered.

"You can help me take care of the herd."

For the first time, a smile lit up Austin's face.

Mrs. Derrick looked relieved. "I'm sorry your father and I are away so much. But running away isn't the answer. We were so terribly worried."

"I know." Austin looked as though he knew how much worry he had caused them and was truly sorry.

To lessen the tension, Grandfather said lightly, "I thought you kids weren't going to find a mystery here!"

"One found us anyway," Henry said, grinning.

Everyone looked relieved and a bit tired after the long, eventful day before and their early morning meeting.

"Grandfather!" Benny cried. "Next time we go on vacation, we *promise* no mysteries!"

The grown-ups laughed heartily at Benny's declaration but Henry, Jessie, Violet, and even Benny wondered silently if it was a promise they would be able to keep.

GERTRUDE CHANDLER WARNER discovered when she was teaching that many readers who like an exciting story could find no books that were both easy and fun to read. She decided to try to meet this need, and her first book, *The Boxcar Children*, quickly proved she had succeeded.

Miss Warner drew on her own experiences to write each mystery. As a child she spent hours watching trains go by on the tracks opposite her family home. She often dreamed about what it would be like to set up housekeeping in a caboose or freight car — the situation the Alden children find themselves in.

When Miss Warner received requests for more adventures involving Henry, Jessie, Violet, and Benny Alden, she began additional stories. In each, she chose a special setting and introduced unusual or eccentric characters who liked the unpredictable.

While the mystery element is central to each of Miss Warner's books, she never thought of them as strictly juvenile mysteries. She liked to stress the Aldens' independence and resourcefulness and their solid New England devotion to using up and making do. The Aldens go about most of their adventures with as little adult supervision as possible — something else that delights young readers.

Miss Warner lived in Putnam, Connecticut, until her death in 1979. During her lifetime, she received hundreds of letters from girls and boys telling her how much they liked her books.